The cover of this book is made with the use of Canva (consisting of a combination of the font Amatic SC and an original background picture).

CONTENTS

THE LAKESHIRE WOODS 1

HE FOLLOWS 9

THE SMILEY CASE..19

MAKE THEM LEAVE 27

I VISITED HILLSBURY 37

ONE BY ONE 42

THE APOCALYPSE HAS BEGUN 50

I SEE THE FUTURE IN MY DREAMS..57

THE OTHER SIDE 61

MISTER BARTON 68

AUTHOR CONTACT 72

THE LAKESHIRE WOODS

THE LAKESHIRE WOODS

Consider this note as a warning. You must listen to me. Don't look for them. Please, don't think of them. For your safety, do not mention them.

Let me start from the beginning.

My name is Michael Cultswich. I am an archeologist working for Barton Industries, a corporation formed in the 60s, which specializes in three global branches, those centering on history, technology, and astronomy. At this exact moment, I am 43 years old. I have... well... I had a lovely wife named Martha, along with my daughter Eva.

Twenty-four days ago, I was sent to the Netherlands and assigned to a research team of four. Now, before I continue, I should tell you the detailed description of my work. I am not a regular archeologist. We are not regular archeologists. What do I mean by this? Regular archeologists want to understand why people lived where they lived, what life might have been like for a group of people, and what changes to their society may have occurred. We, however, want to know why cultures in history failed, what was the reason for their failure, and finally, what brought them down.

They sent me to Duivelsberg, a mountain top surrounded by a thick wide forest. Being located there during the cold winter would not be easy, so I prepared. I packed two fur coats, woolen gloves, a hat, a scarf, and thick rubber boots. The company I worked for prepared the means of my travel. On a cold evening, I arrived by being driven in a private jet. Upon standing there, my new team picked me up, and we drove to our headquarters. Our team was made up of the following participants.

The main scientist was a blonde woman named Jessica Pitchingson. At first glance, she looked like she was a charismatic person.

Her assistant was Mihal Boris. A bearded man, born in Russia. I know it may sound silly, but believe me. He seemed like he could see your darkest secrets just by his gaze. When looking at him, you could feel his frosty glare at any moment.

The third person in the team was our engineer, Martha Glade. She managed all our equipment and made sure it was functional all the time.

My soon to be partner was a young man in his 20s. His name was Andy Hurtshaw. He was a Portuguese expert in tracking, finding what needed to be found. Believe me, he was good at it.

We arrived at what seemed like a small cottage in the middle of the woods. The wind was stiff, and clouds filled the sky. Rain was imminent. The interior of the cottage comprised a wide red sofa, two wooden chairs, and a fireplace. Dark wooden walls surrounded us. As we entered, Jessica greeted me with a handshake.

She spoke in a welcoming tone. "We are all glad to have you here with us, Michael. I understand you don't know all the fine details, but we'll keep you on track. Our team was sent here after Barton Industries received a report of fossils being found by the locals in this area. The fossils were located in the Duivelsberg cave. However, these fossils resembled no features of the prehistoric man. This is what they meant."

She held a skull the shape of a human, but between its teeth which seemed ordinary enough, there were three long fangs. It seemed unnatural. The fangs almost stretched to the upper jaw. And inside, there was one hole in the upper part where there would be the flesh, most likely serving the use of providing space for the fangs when the mouth had been closed, and there were two others in the bottom as well.

"That's where they went in." I spoke as I examined the skull.

The others stared at me. Jessica responded. "Yes. You see why this seems… unfitting."

Boris approached. He held what seemed like a hair in his right hand. "This is what has us worried." The piece was long, the color dark brown. I quickly placed the thought in my head together.

"That can't be…" I muttered.

He smiled. "The past age of this hair is two days. We have a live sample on our hands."

"Why haven't you informed the company of this? None of this was mentioned in my report."

Jessica answered anxiously. "If we informed them, they would send the Cold Team. Our findings would be lost. Don't you want to know? There is a possibility we can communicate with them."

She held the skull in her hand. "The age is around 4500 thousand years old. Imagine what they could tell us. Look, you just arrived here, sleep on it. We'll decide tomorrow." She patted me on the shoulder as she spoke, a soft smile forming across her lips.

The next morning came quickly. When I woke up, they were already packing the equipment. I rushed up to my feet and dressed in the clothes I've arrived in. They stood by the door, waiting for me.

Boris stood in front of the open door of the cottage, looking at me with a menacing expression. "You're either in or out. Decide now."

What this team was doing was strictly breaking the Barton policy. This was not the first time our colleagues discovered something strange, but all of them informed us. I could have called my operator right there and then, but out of instinct, I decided to follow them, audio recording our conversations.

God… why did I not act then? None of this would've happened…

We walked through the woods, dark oaks surrounding us, bushes filled with thorns, and crunchy grass beneath our steps. The clouds still occupied the skies, thankfully no rain this day. We walked for what seemed like miles, stopping at random intervals. After what seemed like two hours, we saw it. An opening in the mountain.

Martha unpacked a suitcase she had been carrying. She took a drone out, handing the remote to Andy. He drove the device into the darkness of the cave. All of us stared at the video feed.

Jessica sighed. "Good. We're clear."

As if knowing I was going to ask, Boris spoke. "The day before you arrived, the day we discovered the sample, a wild boar was inside. Thankfully, we handled the fucker."

As we entered the opening, darkness engulfed us. Martha lit a flare. The red light enabled us to see. Rows of unbalanced rocks stood around, spikes which looked as they could fall any moment above us. At first view, I could only see the rock walls in front, but Martha fixed my sight quickly. She and the rest of the team walked to the right corner of the cave, crouched. As I walked over, I could see a small opening, which led to God knows where.

Andy smiled at me. "This is where we found them, right here in front of the passage."

Jessica quickly laid down and turned on the light on her yellow helmet.

"Now, we're going in!" She excitedly said.

"Wait!" I yelled. "That seems awfully small."

Boris bumped me on the shoulder. "We'll break through, one way or the other."

One by one, we all entered the opening. I lied behind Martha, as we continued squeezing through, Andy behind me. The passage was tight. My shoulders hit the deformed rocks constantly, my legs feeling as if they were tied by a rope, one pressed against the other. At one point, I felt stuck, couldn't move forward, a large rock pressed against my back. Slowly but surely, I started to panic, yelling. "Hey! Hey! I'm stuck!" Jessica's voice could be heard. "Breathe slowly! Relax your muscles!" I gasped for air, but listened to her. After a moment, I squeezed onwards.

"I'm out!" Jessica yelled, which gave us all the confidence to continue. Martha and Boris also made it out, I and Andy were left. As I was making my way towards the exit, Andy screamed. "Um, people! Something's behind me!" Due to not being able to turn around, I asked him. "What do you mean?"

"I mean, something's touching my legs! It's scratching me!" Upon hearing his reply, a chill ran through me. I rushed on forward, and when I made my way out, the three of us were waiting for him. He was still crying in pain. As we saw his arm, we grabbed it immediately. When we pulled him out, we took a look at him. His right leg looked normal, but his left leg… It had long, deep scratches on it. Martha quickly pulled out a first aid kit from her bag and wrapped the wound. Boris quickly looked inside the opening we passed through, shining his flashlight. "There's nothing there. Are you sure you didn't scratch through rock?" Andy looked at him, shock and fear running through his face. "No, something was scratching me!" He trembled from pain. Martha offered him a painkiller, which he gladly took.

I could see it right there and then, the look on Boris's face. A look of utter confusion, but hidden by the posture of his shoulders and the look of his sharp eyes. We stood in a large cavernous area. Small drops of water were dripping from the spikes above us. We all spread out and looked around the new area we found ourselves in. I can't remember when, but at one point, Martha yelled for us. We walked towards her in the eastern part of the area. Once we stood beside her, we were just as amazed as she was. We were standing on an edge, pure darkness beneath us. Our flashlights couldn't even remotely brighten it up. Instead, the light which they cast was swallowed by the dark. Jessica picked up a small rock and threw it down. Nothing could be heard. Boris threw a larger rock. From what I could guess back then, two full minutes passed, and just as we were going to turn around, we heard it crack.

"What the hell?" Andy bewilderedly spoke. Without answering, I nodded. This made little sense. For an object to hit the ground in two minutes, the depth would have to be... God, I can't even comprehend how long. Martha was unzipping her bag and taking out the drone when suddenly, the ground began to shake. We dashed away from the edge, and as we did so, spikes began to fall. We rushed toward the passage we squeezed through. That is when our worst fear came to reality. The passage was shut by the fallen rocks inside it. The shaking stopped, and we were left there, alone in the dark.

The smile from Jessica's face was gone, and Boris's confidence dwindled. He got up on his feet, and picked up Martha's bag, opening it.

"How do you turn it on?" He spoke furiously as he held the drone with his right hand, the remote with his left.

Jessica tried to calm him down, but was met with his furious yelling. Eventually, Martha turned on the device. Boris was slowly calming down. "Look, every entrance must have an exit. Our only way forward is down there." The others slowly nodded as he spoke. He motioned for us to follow him. All of us stood on the edge as Martha lowered the drone below. Our eyes were fixated on the live feed.

At first, nothing but darkness could be seen. Then suddenly, another crack was heard. We were sure the drone landed as we were viewing what appeared to resemble the floor, but... but this... A shock ran through us. The floor was not that of a cave. Quite contrary, the drone stood on black tiles, like those you'd find in a kitchen. All of them were neatly placed. The ground was flat. That's

7

when we saw it. Someone or something was running toward the drone! Martha was unable to lift the device on time, as it was already standing in front of it. The feet... they were human. Long, unchipped nails, unshaven skin filled with hair. They were tapping. Whatever it was that stood in front of the drone had suddenly picked it up! All of us were frozen, waiting for what would come next. After a short walk, we were viewing a door, similar to the ones you'd find in your homes. A wooden front surface with a golden handle. I could see it. Jessica thought of yelling, but as she saw what was next, she stopped in motion. Once the door had opened, the device was placed on a wooden shelf of a small room. The black walls were perfectly flat. What we saw next filled all of us with dread. The floor was filled with... bones, human bones... The other walls also had shelves. Glass jars were placed on them, filled with blood In the middle of the room, a black bowl was placed. Placed inside it... were eyes. The video feed was engulfed in darkness whatever picked the device up had closed the door.

Now, we are sitting next to each other. We hear the small crumbling of rocks as... whatever it is... is climbing up...

HE FOLLOWS

HE FOLLOWS

"Oh, God! Do... does anyone hear me?!? We... I am Birlingham Island! I... We don't have a lot of time left! Please, send help!"

"Sir, I want you to calm down. You have reached an officer of the Police Department of-"

"He... he is here..."

"Sir, who is there? Can you describe your surroundings? In what part of Birlingham Island are you located? Hello?"

"God... I don't know... We're... Yes, we're in Hardley's Park. In a cave system beneath. Please, send help!"

"Two units are on their way, sir. What I need from you is to describe to me what had occurred to you? What is going on, and most important of all... If you are in any kind of imminent danger, I need you to be quiet and to wait for the officers who are on their way."

"He... he left... I, I will tell you everything. Just please, do not abandon me."

THE FOLLOWING EVENTS TOOK PLACE ON SEPTEMBER 9th, 2011.

"My name... my name is Michael Lanchester. I work as an assistant in Barton Industries. I... I and the people who work in our section were sent... were sent on a vacation that had been paid by the upper levels from our company as a reward for... for our hard work."

Seconds of silence filled the line before the voice would be heard once more.

"The destination of our trip was Birlingham Island, and… and we were set to stay there for a period spanning across two weeks. We… we were sent by a yacht, which also had been paid by the upper levels. In fact, everything was paid prior to our departure, the residence, the drive, all our accommodating features."

"When did you arrive, sir?"

"On September 2nd."

"A week before now?"

"Yes, a week before. The men and women who traveled with me were… oh God. Veronica Reeland, she was our manager. Thomas Cole was the janitor at our department level. Jacobs… Jacobs Lancaster, he was our… our overlooker. Stella Zovanovich was our connection with the public, and there… there were…"

"Sir, yes? You can continue, sir. Hello?"

"I hear you, but… I cannot tell their names. Oh God. He's close…"

"Sir? Hello?"

Jeffrey Styles had turned around to address the people who were stationed around him, many of who were listening in on the conversation. The inner blue-colored ceiling's lights shined on his forehead, on which drops of sweat had accumulated.

Not waiting for their questions, he immediately spoke to the secretary, who stood next to his captain. "Sheila, I need you to trace the location of this call right now, and I need it to be made as accurate as can be possible. Understand?"

Without a word, the young brunette walked outside of the small square room, whose three walls of grey displayed the humid drops on their surface, ones that resembled the still-falling rain from the outside, whose cold drops of water consistently fell on the window in front of his wooden desk.

The old man who stood in front of him, his captain, Richard Weasley, now spoke, a grim tone escaping his words. "You are doing alright, Styles. I just need you to follow to do so. Can you do that?"

Still thinking about the sudden task he was assigned with, Jeffrey looked at the woman who stood next to Richard, whose upper right side of her black suit was decorated by the logo of her employer.

BARTON INDUSTRIES: ELIMINATIONS

Without a moment's notice, she addressed the detective.

"Mr. Styles, what we need from you is to discover what had occurred on the island. Our units are on their way."

Drops of sweat were sliding on the skin of his forehead, as Jeffrey had still been just as surprised as his captain before him because of the sudden arrival of the woman standing next to them. The inner walls of the police station were now decorated with hundreds of wires spanning from room to room, as several armed men bearing the same logo walked through them, rifles in their hands.

Before he could nod, Jeffrey heard the voice of the man on his headphones once more, whose call itself seemed to be expected by the unknown people around him.

"He's, he walked away again. Look, I do not have a lot of time left. I… I don't want to die, please."

Upon hearing his words, Jeffrey focused his attention on the task set before him and attempted to ease the man's sense of fear. "Listen to me, Michael. Everything is going to be okay, our…"

His eyes met with the woman.

"Our officers are on their way to the island, but in order to find your exact location, we need to have a roadmap that can direct us to what had occurred. Do you understand, Michael?"

He took a piece of paper from underneath his desk and prepared the pen he now held with his left hand.

"Michael, I need you to repeat to me the names of everyone who was on their way to the island with you. Can you do that?"

As if feeling the close tone of his voice, the man answered.

"Okay, I'll tell you everything. With me… were the men and women I worked with, so…"

Jeffrey could hear the trembling breath coming from the other line.

"Veronica Reeland, she… she was the manager of our department. I guess you could tell that she was the one who… who had assigned all the incoming tasks to each of us."

"The closest in line to her was Jacobs… Jacobs Lancaster, who, as I had told you before, was our overlooker. His task, although we did not know to which extent, but we figured he was the one who would assess the results we would achieve with every one of our tasks, and… and pass them to the upper levels."

"Stella Zovanovich, she… she was the one who would interpret our relations to the local public of London, and most important of all, she would keep our affairs safe from their eye."

"Now, the one we were surprised to be with us on our vacation was Thomas Cole, since all we held him as, and frankly speaking, what his job had comprised... was nothing more but... but to clean the mess we would leave behind. You know, stacks of papers and files from our case files."

Jeffrey Styles turned back to look at the woman, who had also listened to the incoming audio through a wirelessly connected earphone. As their eyes met, she waved her hand in the forwarding direction, implying for him to continue.

"He... Hello? Are you there?"

Styles knew something was not right, but continued upon feeling there would be no time for his questions to be answered as of now.

"Yes, I am with you, Michael. Continue, you said there were others. Can you describe further to me?"

"God... alright, I don't care anymore. There were three others with us. They, they worked under a different section of Barton Industries, and to be honest with you, our section did not have any relations with theirs except, except for our last completed task before our departure."

"Do you know their names, Michael?"

"Yes, James Sheppard, a veteran who... who we learned had served for the United States Military for the span... for three decades. Two brothers, Paulie and Chamlee Xang. Except for their names, I... I know little more, since they do not speak our language. The only piece of information I know is that they are from and had been working under Sheppard in China."

As the man had stopped speaking, Jeffrey pursued after, trying to deduct the present situation of the caller.

"Okay, Thomas. Now, what I will need from you is to tell me, how did you find yourself there? Can you tell me what happened on your vacation?"

The woman who had stood behind the detective silently called for one of the armed officers to walk closer, and after a few of her hand gestures, the man connected what seemed to be a typewriter to a small device, on whose plastic frame two green lights were blinking. As soon as the caller spoke, the officer typed each of his words.

"God, it was simple. We arrived by a pre-arranged yacht, which…"

A soft, but notable chuckle could be heard from the other side.

"Which was quite a pleasant arrangement, as we were treated like rich nobles with the expensive drinks and food we would receive. Once the small ship had closed in on the island, we were dropped off and were following Sheppard, who was walking with Veronica side by side."

"Okay, you arrived on the island, and were now walking. Where?"

"To our place of stay. God, it was incredible."

"Describe it to me, Michael."

"It was the Bewoly Mansion. You yourself could have heard of it. A large, L-shaped wooden construction, one where only the rich were to live during their holidays. I and Thomas both held looks of surprise upon seeing the luxurious interior. The inside pool, sofas, and chairs made from the skin of bears, lights that had changing colors built inside of them, more than king-size beds which were each accompanied by a bottle of red wine placed onto them, wide televisions placed all throughout the mansion, fur-covered…"

The woman who stood behind Styles pointed a paper card in his direction, which had the words "red wine" written on it, implying for him to ask about it.

"Michael, I'm going to have to cut you off a bit, but the wine. You said there were bottles of red wine placed on each of your beds. Am I correct?"

"Um, yes. Why do you ask?"

Looking back at her, the woman gestured for him to press on further while she could be seen directing one of her officers.

"I just want to know exactly what you found when you arrived. Continue, Michael, what happened after you settled in?"

"The night we first laid down, I thought I could hear a noise coming from the outside, arriving through the open window in my upper floor bedroom. I… I couldn't make out what it was, as it had seemed to resemble metal scratching against something, but now I know."

A moment of silence found itself between them, as Michael would continue once more.

"For the first four days, everything seemed to be okay, but that is what we were led to believe, as, during the evening periods, Sheppard and the two brothers would not be with us and would return exactly at 9 in the night. Veronica asked them to tell the reason for their three-hour absence, and the old man harshly replied we are not to question them, to which we noticed her unsettled pose."

"What happened on the fifth day, Michael?"

A soft sound of crying was heard before Jeffrey would hear the man's reply.

"Thomas went missing. We... we searched for him around and inside the mansion throughout the day, but... but found no trace. God, I remember it so clearly..."

"What do you remember?"

"Stella, at exactly seven in the evening, when twelve hours had passed since his disappearance, was preparing to call the headquarters and inform them. But..."

"But what?"

"But, Sheppard, he, he took the phone straight from her hands and smashed it against the floor, yelling at both her and us to not dare to call back..."

Seconds of silence passed, and as Jeffrey was about to call for Michael, the young man's voice spoke.

"That's when all hell broke loose. Veronica and Jacobs exchanged yells with the three men, asking for an explanation. I searched for my phone, opening all of my brought bags, checking in my bedroom as the yelling had seemed to escalate to an even higher level, now coming from both sides, but... but I couldn't find it anywhere. I walked back downstairs, and was about to interfere with the argument myself, but... but that's when it happened..."

"Go on, Michael."

"A hit. A damn hit was heard against the sliding glass door we all had stood by, the wide doors of glass which led to the even wider living room we all were standing in. It was him, Thomas. He was hung by a piece of rope that... that had been tied to the angled roof of the mansion. His teeth were, oh God..."

"They were pulled out, all of them."

"What did you do after?"

17

"At that same moment, Sheppard and the two men ran upstairs, practically throwing themselves inside their rooms. Stella and I looked to Veronica for guidance, but she was silent as the three men walked outside, dressed in full military vests, each of them having a heavy-duty rifle with them. The... the reason she was silent was because of the logo attached to the upper left part of their vests..."

BARTON INDUSTRIES: ELIMINATIONS

Quiet, but ever so lightly heard sobbing was coming from Michael, to which Jeffrey was to push on further.

"Michael, where are they?"

"Dead, every single one of them, except for me"

"He is outside, waiting for me. He... he has no eyes..."

Jeffrey began to speak harshly, "Michael, continue, tell me what happened after. Michael?"

The sound of a wooden door opening was heard, and four steps echoed throughout the call, each of them coming closer.

"Tell the woman who is by your side. Tell Elizabeth that... he follows..."

THE SMILEY CASE

THE SMILEY CASE

Greetings, my name is Marcus Folley. I am a detective working for the police department of Hillsbury. Look, I am not a man who likes to write, moreover, I can safely say I hate writing all kinds of notes. But, there is a reason I am writing these letters. They are for you. In case I don't come back.

So, where do I begin? There is much to tell. Let us start in the past two months. Our police department deals with many cases here in England, and many of those can range from plain out silly to haunting. Over the last ten years, I've slowly advanced through the rankings in the system, going from a rookie to a detective. Huh, I guess I've got only one or two promotions left to reach the top.

For your sake and the sake of others, I want to tell you in which month these letters were written, in case I truly do disappear. September 2005.

On the 3rd of July, while I and my partner Wallace were driving to the nearby donut shop, our unit asked for us through the radio speaker. Wallace, being a pain in the ass he usually is, called our station through his cellphone, telling them we'll be late, that we are dealing with suspicious activity in the street shops, which was an obvious lie of his. As he spoke out of our excuse, his lips formed a serious expression a few seconds after. Taking his phone away from his ear and putting it in his pocket, he silently told me to drive to our new destination. I asked him what was going on since I was not used to seeing him hopping on to cases the moment they're called. Wallace slowly shifted his gaze to me, the coldness emanating from his eyes.

Wallace: "It's Patrick, Marc. He's the victim."

As I heard the words escaping his mouth, I stepped on the pedal as fast as I could. Confusion ran through my mind. Patrick was our connection with the Bureau, our connection with the States.

20

Little time passed until our arrival at the scene. I, Wallace, and nine of our colleagues from the department stood there, viewing what awaited us. The coroners surrounded the body, each carrying a plastic bag, dressed in all white, blue gloves on their hands. Patrick... God, it was horrifying to see.

He lied there on the floor, both his hands and feet spread wide like he was playing in the snow. His mouth was pulled to both sides, forming an unnatural smile. His stomach was ripped open, like some animal had eaten right through it. But there was something there, something inside. The coroner cut through the stomach, which was pulled upwards, distinguishing it from the other organs. As his small blade slit through it, we could see an item. A tape.

We were standing in a blind alley. Patrick was lying right in front of the wall at the end. No doors surrounded us. I don't know what it was, but something did not give me peace until I jumped to the other side of the tall wall in front. Wallace yelled after me, calling me back, and as seconds passed, I heard him running around the street to me. I was standing on the other side of the wall, which could have been crossed over if Patrick had used force to jump and grab the top with his hands, dragging himself across, as I did. I was right to do so, you see, as I and Wallace, who slowly walked to me, his eyes and mouth wide, saw it.

A large, red-painted smiley face was drawn on the other side of the wall, on the other side where Patrick was found. Wallace quickly yelled for our colleagues and coroners to run to us and seal the area. During that moment, he and I, our eyes crossed several times, looks of silence, looks of worry. This event had to be kept hidden from the public, who would panic knowing a serial killer was walking in the streets.

As Wallace and I met the painting staring at us, we knew what we faced. The red color, it was blood, Patrick's blood. The shape of the painting, the iconic dragging of the lines, we knew, and we knew well. Over the previous five years, murders ran through England. All of them could not have been solved, as no biological or relatable evidence was found. It was as if all the victims were killed out of the blue when they least expected it. Some were found in their beds, throats sliced. Some were hung on the walls, deep, large bolts running through their arms and legs. And some were left hanging on rope, beaten like mere dogs. All of them, however, left the same sign, the same brand. A smiley face.

Wallace slightly chuckled as he was looking at the floor.

Wallace: "Fucking hell. It had to have been us, Marc. We had to witness his new… his new way of leaving his goddamn presents."

Suddenly, my phone rang. It was our captain, Jacobs.

Jacobs: "Marcus, I am going to need you and Wallace in my office as soon as possible."

Marcus: "Yes, of course, captain."

I spoke as I hung up, Wallace eyeing me.

Wallace: "What'd he say?"

Marcus: "He needs us, and he needs us quickly."

We drove through the streets of Hillsbury. Clouds engulfed the sky, drops of rain sliding across the windows of our car. We greeted our colleagues as we were entering the headquarters of our station, walking up to the captain's office, who was standing away from us as we entered, staring at the city from the enormous glass wall. He slowly turned around and motioned for us to sit, a grim look on his face.

Jacobs: "By now, you must have already guessed why I called you here, detectives. We are dealing with a delicate case. Look, I was informed by our contacts from the Bureau that we have no jurisdiction here. Several teams of their branch are driving to our location from other parts of Europe as we speak."

He pressed his hands to his knees. Sweat ran across his forehead.

Jacobs: "Did I make myself clear, gentlemen?"

He asked as he wiped his forehead with a tissue.

Wallace and I nodded in agreement as our eyes ran across each other. Heavy rain poured outside. Thunder could be heard. As we got up from the chairs, the captain's assistant ran inside, panic running through her.

Jessica: "Captain! You have to come outside!"

Jacobs: "What is it now, Jessica?"

Jessica: "Quickly!"

Slowly, but surely, all of us followed the assistant to the outside. We stood in front of the entrance to the station, looking around ourselves.

Jacobs: "What, Jessica?"

The scared assistant was trembling with fear. She pointed her finger upwards. And a sight surely did await us. Just as I saw it next to Patrick, a smiley face was painted right beneath the roof of the building, a sentence beneath it.

"I WANT YOU. ALL OF YOU!"

Jacobs quickly yelled: "Oh God, send someone up there immediately! Wallace, send a team to look around the building this moment!"

All the searching efforts were futile, as the person responsible had disappeared earlier, leaving us to ponder. I remember it clearly, the moment I and Wallace were standing next to the coroners who had cleaned the tape, our captain beside us. The words we heard sent chills down all of our spines, names, surnames. The tape had spoken all the names and surnames of the people working in the department, their home addresses following, and leaving a message at the end.

"SEE YOU SOON!"

Jacobs scratched his head with both his hands, trying to hide the fury building inside him. Wallace, on the other hand, smiled while looking at Patrick, who was lying on the metal desk. I looked at him, unsure of the reason for his behavior. Then he looked at me, speaking.

Wallace: "Fucking hell. We have a mole in our ranks."

He looked at Jacobs.

Wallace: "With all due respect, captain, I'm going to equip myself. I suggest you do, too."

Wallace motioned for me to follow him. As we left the building, he gave me a large military knife, along with a pistol. I looked at him, bewildered, which led him to speak once more.

Wallace: "Just keep this in your house. Be safe, partner."

He spoke as he tapped me on the shoulder, walking into the streets. This killer, he has not been caught for several years now, but I knew there was no way in hell he could take out an entire police department. There were men with military backgrounds, folks who fought in wars, others who worked for the countless government agencies. They had nothing to worry about! This must have been something to set us off, to make us focus on other things and goals as the man responsible would slip away. Unfortunately, all it took was two weeks.

The calls started coming in. Day by day, more of my colleagues were found dead, murdered in several brutal ways, each having a smiley face painted close to them. They were found in numerous places around the city, all the way from streets to fucking schools! The captain issued out a warning for all of us to stick together, asking us to share our homes. We began splitting into groups of two, I and Wallace moving into my house, sleeping on couches. The ones with families, well, they got used to it somehow. After all, the process was supposed to last for only a couple of days.

But it did not help, however, as more and more murders started arriving, multiple families slaughtered beyond imagination! We checked the order of the names spoken on the tape, and indeed, the killings followed the list. I and the captain tried to find the next name on the list, and it was Wallace. We searched for him at the station, called the officers in town, but it was as he had perished! A few minutes later, we received a call from a citizen saying he had seen a man lying on the road in the outskirts of the city. It was Wallace. He had not been taken care of there, no. His body was dumped on the road. He was killed somewhere else. We found a card placed next to him, a smiley face painted on it, and beneath it, my name was written.

As the ongoing weeks passed, we finally met the team of the Bureau who had arrived to help us out. The agents had taken care of keeping things secret, as the local news reported nothing that was going on. I... I still cannot get my head around it! How could one man take out several trained detectives and officers? We were not the primary station in London, I know. We were a small station responsible for the city of Hillsbury, on the outskirts of London. Even so, there was no explanation I could provide for what was going on! Some cases we witnessed looked dreadful. It got to a point that we were seeing arms and legs torn off of human bodies, but there was no sign of forced entry! The doors were locked from the inside, as suggested by the captain. As I read my name on the card, I quickly rushed to my house and checked every inch I could find. Then, as I did so, I locked all the doors and windows. Luckily, I had cameras placed around my house, enabling me to see my surroundings from the inside. The agents of the Bureau were sitting in the vans parked in front of my house and around the streets.

However, several days passed by. An entire month had passed, and I began returning to work, catching up with my responsibilities on the job. The agents of the Bureau found a lead pointing them to New York, a woman killed in her flat, her throat sliced, a smiley face on the wall next to her. Yesterday, I visited Wallace's grave. The clouds filled the sky. Rain poured down on me

25

as I let out tears of guilt. If only I was there with him. The reason I am writing you these letters revolves around an event that occurred to me this very evening. I sat in my living room, watching the daily news as an alarm buzzed on my security system. One of the cameras caught something, to be more precise, the camera in front of my door.

A man was standing there. He wore a mask made from skin, patches of human skin sewed together, forming a smiley face. He waved to me.

It is close to midnight as of this moment. I am holding the knife and pistol Wallace gave me while I am crouching behind the door of my bedroom, waiting.

If you ever encounter murders similar to this one, you need to follow what I write here. Run, and don't look back!

MAKE THEM LEAVE

MAKE THEM LEAVE

I presume the following text that is about to be read had been written on November 3rd, 2014. The events described inside are not to be taken as evident facts, because many of the mentioned circumstances are still in the phase of further research conducted by Barton Industries: Secret Operations.

Signed, sealed, and set under the High Classification Database.

Jeff Sayers.

BARTON INDUSTRIES: SECRET OPERATIONS

For everyone who may find these notes, I send my dearest regards, Farhad Asanhum.

For my introduction, I wish you to not search for long, as none of my past and present time spent matters anymore. They are here. They have been watching us for so... so long. They have looked after us. They have guided us. They are among us.

For you to understand the words you are about to read, the words I have written for, whoever may find them, I wish them to be taken with the utmost care.

As was written before, my name is Farhad Asanhum. I am what some would call a lifelong searcher across the stars. Ever since I had learned to speak, I always looked up and wondered. What else is there among us?

I have spent the last twenty-seven years with two people who I hold to be the dearest of a family I could ever imagine. Their names are as follows.

Afsharid Lenkansir, who, currently, is fifty-two years of age. For how little I am allowed to write, Afsharid has faithfully served NASA, The National Aeronautics and Space Administration. For more than fifteen years, and ever since discovering what I had shown him, he has been my faithful companion in discovering the truth of life itself.

And then, there is Leila Arhenshaw, a woman I have met when I was just seventeen years old, as, in that time of my life, I was sent to a college institution established in the Netherlands. It is that factor of "choice" that has led me to meet her, the love of my life.

She is the love that has followed me ever since, the love that has given up on her dreams, all in order to help me reach those dreams. Leila is the love that is with me now.

There is so much I could write to you, so many points in our lives I would so gladly share, but alas, there is no time to do so, as I am awaited.

The events I now write of occurred on the 26th of October, 2014.

In the briskness of night, I was awoken from my sleep, Leila still sleeping next to me. Upon finding the source of the sound I've heard, I opened up my flip phone, and the number that was calling me was none other than that of Afsharid, who, at the time, I presumed to be in Beirut, working on a satellite dish that had been in the process of construction by the company he still had worked for.

"Friend, are you there?"

At first, the tone that spoke to me, his tone, I recognized to be the one of a certain unease.

"Always, friend. Tell me, what do you need of me?"

For a second, a glitching sound erupted between our two lines, after which I heard him.

"Are you alone?"

I smiled for a bit, after which I answered.

"Alone as can be. Leila's by my side."

No sound would arrive after my reply, and as I was about to hang up the call in order to call him back, he spoke back.

"Both of you, listen to me carefully. What I need you to do now as quickly and as best as you can is to pack your radio signaling equipment, and… and walk outside. There will be four men, all of them dressed in black uniforms, glasses concealing their eyes, waiting for you."

"Hold on, friend."

"There is no time, Farhad." Suddenly, he spoke firmly.

"You need to enter the vehicle with them, after which you will be driven to a remote location outside New York, where you will be escorted to a private plane that will fly you to my destination."

I was, honest to God… I was about to ask him so much more, but there I was, in the hurriedness of it all, quickly waking Leila up and telling her to pack our things immediately.

Walking outside of our small home, we saw them, four of them, standing there, waiting for us, without a word spoken.

The drive itself had begun the moment we entered and as the door was closed by one of the two men who sat with us in the back, the remaining two entered and sat in the front. The time that had passed until we arrived was dead silent.

You might find this funny, but I was checking, closely listening with my ears in order to differentiate, in… in order to recognize the sound of breathing coming from, at the very least, one of them.

But, but there were none. They stared blankly in front, no sound, nor the sight of them breathing in or out.

Now I know that even then, they had been with us!

We arrived at the location where indeed, a small, but luxurious-looking small grey plane had been stationed, going through desolate roads that had no cement placed on the rocks and dirt which they comprised, ending up next to the aircraft, in a small open patch between the thickness of the surrounding woods.

Just as it had happened before, once we had entered the plane, there was no time to rest, as the craft had turned on its engines. Inside, we sat on two large, comfortable chairs made of light yellow leather. Between us, on a glass table, two pills of blue had been placed.

Next to them, a small white envelope was placed, and upon opening it, we were told to drink the pills, which, as if on cue, had been made possible to be consumed, as one of the two pilots walked back into our small space, stepping through the open passage leading into the control room.

The man did not reveal his face, as a grey helmet had been placed over his head, and when he gave us two bottles of water, he walked back, sitting next to who we presumed was his co-pilot. The men who were present with us before could now be seen through the small, round windows around us. They had entered the vehicle and were driving off.

After drinking the pills, our vision had turned to an unexplained blurriness, as we both had seemed to fall asleep. The next sight that would await me was none other than Afsharid himself, who was crouching in front of me, holding his hand out. Upon fully opening them... my eyes... I could see I was lying down in a small, square-shaped room, where the walls, ceiling, and floor had both been made of white tiles.

Lying down next to me was Leila, who was now beginning to wake up as well.

"Friend, get up and walk with me. Okay?"

He spoke to me with a gentle tone coming from him, as his lips were smiling. Taking his hand, I stepped up, and we were now beginning to walk, but… but before we continued, I turned back to Leila, who was still slowly regaining her consciousness.

"Should we not wait for her, Afsharid?"

"She will be joining us soon, Farhad. You can be sure of that."

He answered back, as I felt a small sense of tension building up between us. I… I do not know where we were located, because as we were walking forward, I was shocked to see the environment surrounding me.

From what I could count, there were dozens of men and women walking around the enormous spaces of white, each of them dressed in a scientific robe, all of them bearing the sign.

BARTON INDUSTRIES: RESEARCH SECTOR

I could see long glass tanks that seemed to be filled with a green liquid of some kind. They were attached to the right and left walls, almost… almost filling them in their entirety, all of them connected by small glass tubes passing through each one.

Some of the people were writing down notes on, from what I could see, were already overly filled sheets of paper. Some were standing in front of the tanks, looking upwards while exchanging words that could not be heard during my presence. But... but there were others who... who just did not seem right.

They... they looked as if they were in some sort of trance. In front of each stood two to three of the other scientists, who were touching their necks, as if they had been looking for a pulse. But... but the people were just standing there, with... with wide smiles present on their faces.

Suddenly, I was pulled out of my state, as Afsharid spoke to me while we stood in front of what seemed to be a metal door, above which the following letters were written.

SECTION 5A/1

"Farhad, what I need from you now is to listen, and to listen carefully."

He spoke as he eyed me carefully, a look of uncertainty coming from his eyes.

"Of course, Afsharid."

I answered, waiting for him to continue speaking.

"Behind these doors is a specimen. To be more clear, a specimen we discovered in the near depths of the North-eastern region of the Atlantic Ocean. The impacting reason for our discovery were the scans we were receiving from the satellites that were stationed above this particular region. The readings themselves appeared to show an object which passed through our orbit at a speed we have yet to achieve."

He stopped for a moment, as he looked to be calculating his next words.

"Upon our arrival, we discovered the craft, which was broken down into three parts. That craft is being examined in Nevada as we speak. Behind these doors, Farhad... is its passenger."

"Passenger?" I spoke with confusion, but before I would receive an answer, a man and a woman wearing scientific robes approached us, handing us both helmets coated in black. Afsharid continued to speak.

"Farhad, all the people who are currently standing behind these doors are ordered to be wearing these particle-obstruction helmets, and I need you to follow these rules so to avoid any anomalies that may come our way."

Hearing him, I immediately placed the helmet on, and as I did so, my vision was now partially blurred, my sight becoming surrounded by a purplish color.

We entered, and what awaited me was... was... was something I could never imagine or clearly describe. Nine of us stood, and in front of us, from what could be seen through the helmet itself, was what appeared to be a glass wall, behind... behind which... it stood.

The creature... it appeared to have two upper and lower limbs. Its head was abnormally round, through which small spikes seemed to be pushed upwards. The body itself... was... was crooked, skin pushed so close to its bones, arms which, instead of fingers, had nothing, but a circular end... legs... more rather tentacles, as the two lower limbs ended on what I could only describe as a tail. But... but its eyes, they... they were gone... nothing but hollow shells inside the three openings on its head. It... it had no mouth.

Even though there seemed to be no way of doing so, I heard it speak to me, in... in such a clear voice.

"WE ARE HERE. WE ARE ALL HERE."

I know that the reason for my arrival, the reason Afsharid had intended, was for me to help them examine it, to help them try to identify its cellular levels, as I had done before on suspicious entries for the last six years.

"JOIN US. BECOME ONE."

But... but I couldn't handle it, as I had suddenly thrown the helmet from my head, and was now having a clear vision of what stood before me. It... it was... it was beyond any possible ability to be explained. But... it was beautiful.

In mere seconds, Afsharid pushed me to the ground, yelling at me in unison with the men and women around him for making the action I did.

Now, I am writing to you from a room I have been escorted to, and I was told that Afsharid, together with Leila, will come to see me soon.

But nothing matters anymore!

I HEAR THEM! I HEAR THE VOICES! THEY ARE CALLING FOR ME! THEY CALL FOR ME TO BECOME ONE WITH THEM! AND... AND I WILL! THEY TELL THE TRUTH! THEY TELL ME EVERYTHING ABOUT US... ALL OF US! I... I THINK I NOW KNOW... THE MEANING OF LIFE!

PRESENT REPORT

PATIENT FARHAD ASANHUM HAS BEEN PLACED INSIDE ROOM 304/A12, AND IS NOW UNDER CLOSE EXAMINATION BY THE SCIENTIFIC SECTOR OF BARTON INDUSTRIES.

CURRENTLY, THE PATIENT HOLDS THE FOLLOWING SIDE EFFECTS.

1. THE PATIENT'S BODY TEMPERATURE, EVER SINCE THE CLEAR SIGHT HAD OCCURRED IS STILL CONSISTENTLY GOING DOWN WITH NO SIGNS OF STOPPING.
2. THE PATIENT HAS RIPPED OUT BOTH HIS EYES AND HAS PROCEEDED WITH GOUGING THEM, SECONDS AFTER THE INCIDENT.

3. THE PATIENT, AS HE HAD DONE BEFORE, HAS WILLFULLY AND FORCINGLY PULLED OUT HIS TONGUE, AFTER WHICH HE HAS PROCEEDED TO LIE DOWN ON THE FLOOR.
4. THE PATIENT ROSE UP, AND IMMEDIATELY, HAS BEGUN TO SLAM HIS HEAD AGAINST THE WALL, AFTER WHICH MEMBERS OF SECRET OPERATIONS HAVE ENSURED THE FURTHER LIFE EXPECTANCY BY SEDATING HIM WITH HIGH DOSES OF SLEEP INDUCING INJECTIONS.
5. UPON WAKING UP, THE PATIENT RIPPED HIS EARS WITH THE FORCE OF HIS HANDS, AFTER WHICH HE SLAMMED HIS FINGERTIPS INTO THE CLEAR SKIN OF HIS STOMACH, AN ACTION THAT HAS RESULTED IN THE DEALING OF DEADLY WOUNDS TO HIS INNER ORGANS.

FARHAD ASANHUM: DECEASED

NEXT PATIENT: LEILA ARHENSHAW

I VISITED HILLSBURY

I VISITED HILLSBURY

"I... I stepped inside its borders approximately seven hours ago, and I need help. Please, help me find my way back. If... if anyone is able to hear my signal, for the love of God, save me!"

"Um... hello?"

"He... hello?!? Do you hear me?"

"Well, I am having a bit of trouble in doing so, but yes, I do. Where are you calling from?"

"Oh Angels of The Nine, thank you. Um... I am... I am standing somewhere... somewhere in the woods, the woods around Hillsbury!"

"Hillsbury? Hm, I think I know where that may be. Can you tell me what happened? If you guide me through the events you experienced, I may be able to find your trace."

"Of course! My name is Jared Crenshaw. I am a private investigator who specializes in exploring the occult, and any traces surrounding its presence in rural lands. I... Two days ago, I was called by a number I did not recognize, since instead of where the number was supposed to be displayed, letters informed me an unknown caller was contacting me. I... I answered to a woman. I recognized her voice to belong to an elderly. She spoke to me as if she were in pain, and the words she said implied she was asking for my urgent help, and her safety was not assured."

"I am driving through the roads. I will arrive in approximately ten to fifteen minutes, stranger. Did she say who she was? Did she tell you her name?"

"Yes! Yes, she did! During her tense speech, I quickly asked her for an identification, so I would know who to look for when I arrived. She said her name was Margery, Margery Elderlean, and that she lived in The Old Inn! She told me I will be able to trace its location by the signs leading towards it which were placed throughout the town!"

"Good, stranger. That gives me a waypoint to use. Did you find The Old Inn, and if so, how?"

"I… I did. Although, it was not a serene location to find, because I had to traverse through the town, which seemed… which looked as if it were rotten! I walked through the mud-filled dirt roads, looking at my surroundings. The houses were all made of wood. Their walls were painted in white with dark brown roofs. But at first, taking a closer look at them, the wood was broken as… as if it had been splintered by something that could only be described as… as if a bull or something heavy was repeatedly slamming itself against it! The paint showed clear signs of chipping, and it seemed to be progressively consumed by what could be described as a type of mold. And the roofs, they were filled, and I truly mean, filled by… not by… it was as if roots that were so thick and long had pushed themselves through them, splintering them. Nevertheless, the constructions were miraculously held together with the interconnected pieces of wood."

"What you seem to describe to me, well, it tells me that the town was vacant for quite a while. Did you find anyone living inside them?"

"I searched, honest to God, I did. I called out loud! I was beginning to feel an unease building inside of me while I walked through what seemed to be an empty wasteland! But… but that… that is when I noticed…"

"What? What did you notice?"

"The houses, they, they were all the same. It was as if every house was an identical copy of the other! They all had the same pattern. On the front, a wooden door with a glass top, two square windows on each side, and one small window on the back. Seeing them right there and then, I contemplated if I should turn back, but... but then... I heard it..."

"Lord almighty! Hang on, stranger! I'll be back in a sec!"

.

.

.

"In God's name, a bloody crow struck itself against the windshield. Uh, nevermind. Tell me. What did you hear?"

"A yell. No, that is not what it was. It... it was... a... a blood-curdling scream! The moment I heard it, I ran in its directions, and as I was running through the mud, in the corner of my eye, I saw them, the signs which read The Old Inn. Not long after, I found myself standing in front of it."

"What did it look like?"

"It looked different from the other houses. Its walls were made from a darker kind of wood, which also had shown the same type of rot that I saw moments before. But, its structure, I could not perceive it as being the one of an inn. Moreover, it resembled the look of a manor, or even a mansion. Dozens of windows, I could see them on the two floors above."

"What happened after?"

"The screaming, it was still there, although, it had now become less audible, as if the female voice had lowered its strength. I... I quickly walked inside it, but there was not much to be seen, as the interior inside was empty. You... you have to understand. There was nothing there, and the moment I entered, the screaming stopped!"

"I think I see the sign. Hillsbury, did you say it was? Look, continue talking to me. I'm exiting the car, and I'll find my way to that inn, but I'll need you to tell me what happened after you entered, so that I can navigate from there."

"I... I saw it, in the distance. I saw it, looking at me."

"I am close to the signs directing me to the inn. What did you see?"

"Its skin, it was grey. Its arms, shattered bones pierced through them, its legs looking as if they were bent in half, the broken toes leaning on the wooden floor! And, oh God. Its head, its eyes, they were white! The teeth, there were hundreds of them, all of them sharp as if they had belonged to a piranha! It spoke to me."

"Alright, I'm standing in front of the building. You were right to say that it looks rotten beyond repair. Wait, ou said it spoke? What did it tell you?"

"It... it told me to join it..."

"... Stranger... Where are you?"

"We... we are behind you..."

ONE BY ONE

ONE BY ONE

This is Marcus Jefferson. I am reporting off-duty. The text you are about to read must stay off the record at all costs in order to avoid the potential of a risen disturbance in our sector. The date is currently set to the 19th of February 2019. I will begin by formally introducing myself to the readers of these papers.

As I have written before, my name is Marcus Jefferson. I am an agent working for Barton Industries, a global conglomerate corporation that is present and active in many fields of research and improvements of our country's technological advancements, mostly regarding the field of artificial intelligence. For the past six years, I have been working as a member of one of their underground branches. This branch was held secret until now. Its existence had been slipped into the public view, the cause for the breach being a failed operation which took place in Afghanistan last year, a failed attempt of assassinating a leader of a potential terrorist group which could have presented a future threat for the United States of America. The branch I worked in is now publically known as Barton Industries: Secret Operations. Below, you will find the digitally attached imprint of its signature that is present in the suits of every person working under it.

BARTON INDUSTRIES: SECRET OPERATIONS

As was said before, Barton Industries officially focuses its assets and resources in the extensive fields of research and technological advancements. The before mentioned branch that is now discovered and known only by its name, however, focuses on the field of research that was never conducted before. What do I mean by this, you may ask?

I mean that what I have been doing for the last nineteen years, and what my previous colleagues had been doing long before I had arrived, well, simply told, experiences we found ourselves in were not of this world, but something far, far worse. In the year 2003, I and my colleague Tommy were dispatched to investigate a report in the rural town of Rocheport, Missouri. The briefing we had received mentioned several sightings of something unidentifiable in the water of the nearby river. According to the report, three officers of the local police force went missing after they were last seen to be heading to the location of the river in order to conduct an investigation of these activities. In the report, we found six pictures placed beneath the text, snapshots. Two of these snapshots had shown an image of an enormous shadow supposedly taken from the air, a shadow of something moving beneath the water. The four remaining images featured snapshots of the bloody, previously owned police clothes, each found in a distinct part of the small forest. As we gazed deeply into any bits of information we could find, our eyes were met with the text that was typed out beneath. The entire population of this small town went missing five months ago, and this was supposedly the event that had occurred two weeks before, while the area was still populated by its residents. To keep the story short, once Tommy and I set foot in the area, we were baffled to find no traces of footprints, not a bit of DNA evidence, nothing that could lead us to the potential events that had led to this conclusion. Both of us called the family members of each resident we could find on the internet, and all of them pointed to the same detail. They had received a message which contained the following.

"IT IS COLD IN THE WATER. JOIN US. LET PEACE AND STILLNESS SURROUND YOU."

The mobile devices were located in the respected personalized homes that had belonged to the fitting individuals. However, no such message was found, and no signs of digital traces could be discovered by the technological research departments of Barton Industries, as was written in the report. As we had prepared to walk back from the outskirts of the river to our official vehicle of transportation that was parked at the entrance of the town, Tommy and I heard something. It was as we heard a small rock being thrown into the water. Suddenly, as we turned around, we could catch a glimpse of a small, round circle of waves in the water. No one else was present, as we had made sure to check our surroundings once more before our departure.

Once we had walked back to the vehicle, we found something peculiar in the windshield. The windows of the car were covered in moisture, which was expected because of the murky clouds and the soon-to-begin rain, but right there, on the windshield, a sentence had been formed, looking as if someone had created it by pushing their finger across the window.

"LEAVE US. THE DEAD NEED SLEEP."

This chain of events eventually led to the set-up closure of an oil company whose headquarters were placed near the outskirts of the town and the arrest of its headboard. The individuals who were on trial were sentenced to death by the court. This needed to be done in order to provide a sense of explanation for the public. After Barton Industries reported that no explainable circumstances were to be found, it was up to the Federal Bureau of Investigation to provide an acceptable completed investigation, along with the appropriately told chain of events, as well as the found and arrested culprits. The official report in the media outlets stated that the CEO of the oil company did not receive the consent of the local population for further oil digging operations. In order to clear his company of this problem, he ordered the head staff to insert poisonous amounts of anthrax into the local water facility, which would cause the countless deaths of the innocent men and women who lived their ordinary lives. And as the bodies were taken one by one, they were thrown into a waste disposal pit present in the area. Events like these were to be conducted if our investigations fueled no further explanations of the many events we found ourselves in.

I am not a bad person. If you might think so of me after reading the text above, you need to understand I was simply a man doing his job. There was nothing I could have done in the last nineteen years that would turn the tides of countless events in another direction. This is only one of the undercover operations conducted by Barton Industries, but one that was important to me, as the families of those people needed to know the truth of the events that took place back then. The sole reason you are finding these notes in the first place, Mr. Forrester, is that I have been officially discharged from my duties in the above-mentioned corporation. Last week, I was sent with my squad to investigate the events that had been taking place in the city of New York. I, Tommy Wilderson, Jessica Pitchingson, and Martha Richards were the members of our squad. Over the years, the three of us became essential agents in the countless cases of Barton Industries: Secret Operations. The leader of our squad was the before mentioned Martha Richards, who was the CEO of another company that had been formed by the CIA, naming itself the following.

THE UNION SYNDICATE

By the contents of the report, unwanted signs of activity began to form in the sectors of a newly founded factory in the city, one which was owned by Welshare Industries, another branching company forming itself from the conglomeration of ours. Upon our arrival, we met with the current CEO of this building, Jeff Sayers, who had informed us about the disappearance of one of his employees, an overlooker of the repairing process of their goods, Jake Brownlie. As we walked through the wide corridors of the facility, we were met with his factory manager, a man named Mike Browlury. The first note of information he granted presented what would at first seem as unusual, but regarding the circumstances of the employment of anyone who worked under this sector, it was met with utmost caution. Jeff informed us that the employee in question did not arrive at work today. His whereabouts were quickly set for examination, and no trace of him was found. However, there was one particular detail they did not expect to find. His federal apartment was left almost completely untouched, but in his bedroom, a teddy bear, along with a piece of paper, was found on his bed. When that same piece of paper had been unfolded, it was found to contain pictures of him going several months back, and right at the end, beneath the printed photographs, a bloody painting of a switch was found.

As we heard the description coming from his words, we remembered a case that was eerily similar to what we were possibly dealing with now. That case originated at the end of the 90s, when a man by the name of Phil Barton was kidnapped, nowhere to be seen. He was the mayor of New York, the son of Mr. Barton. On that day, his brother Dan, who was the captain of the New York Police Department, went on a hunt for whatever information he could find. Supposedly, Phil's whereabouts were discovered to be in the Alaima Docks. When this piece of information originated, all available officers were dispatched to arrive at that location as quickly as possible. As the men of the law had surrounded the docks, multiple news reporters stood by the side, having their cameras fixed at the entrance of the warehouse. Once the audio was turned on, Dan Barton yelled for the culprit to come out. After seeing that his request had no answer, the young captain ordered the breach team to gather around the large door of the warehouse. Just as they were ready to perform a breach, the door started opening, but what came out was unexpected. A doll.

It was made of wood. Its head had two white glass eyes, a coloured mouth, which looked like it was drawn with a crayon, and a sharp carrot-like orange nose. It wore a black rounded hat. Attached to its legs were steel frames connected to little boxes. A little microphone was attached to its mouth.

The older member of the younger Barton generation looked closer at the edges of the opened gates, which enabled him to see that there were connected speakers placed above. As everyone stood in silence, the devices were remotely turned on. A voice could be heard. A voice whose spoken sentence would be remembered by generations onward.

"Greetings. You don't know me, but I know you. Mr. Barton, you may come out."

At that very moment, Phil Barton could be seen walking through the doors, having a metal collar around his neck. He looked scared, had bruises and cuts all over him, and was missing a finger on his right arm. The echoing, robotic voice continued.

"For a man of law to do such deeds, well, a true shame. Gentlemen, your adored mayor, Phil Barton, is a two-faced fraud. I know you would like for me to explain, but we don't have the time right now. What you see around his neck is an explosive collar. Each millimeter of its interior is filled with explosive powder. And now, he will die."

The young mayor screamed, panic running through him.

"He killed them all!"

At that moment, the collar exploded. From the left side of the entrance, machine gun turrets rose and fired their bullets.

The first thought that came to our minds was that we were dealing with a copycat, someone obsessed with the history surrounding that harrowing case. But then Jeff Sayers picked up a small bag from a wooden case that was placed in his pocket. A finger was placed inside it, the finger of Phil Barton. We had invested ourselves for the remainder of that day, looking at all video and audio recordings of Jake Brownlie, those that originated over the last year. As we returned to the factory the day afterward, we found out that neither Jeff Sayers nor Mike Browlury showed up for work. Along with them, our colleague Jessica, who had stayed in a hotel the night before, meeting one of her friends from this area, did not return any of our calls. Martha called for both of us to meet her in an undisclosed area she had occupied for the last twenty-four hours. As I and Tommy arrived, we were told by her to not disclose any point of these events with our sector in Barton Industries. However, Tommy refused to obey, saying he had made a call to our squad informant, Patrick Weasley, asking for his arrival, with further explanation to follow. Upon hearing his words, she picked up a pistol from her left pocket, firing a bullet through his head.

I stood in silence, sudden shock running through me. Martha ordered me to clean the area and said to meet her in my previous whereabouts when I had finished. I placed down two incendiary grenades, one beside the door, the other beside Tommy. While I was walking out, I pushed the button on the black remote, feeling the sudden warmth of flames and hearing the sound of burning wood behind me. As I walked up to my car, I calculated about informing the authorities present in Secret Operations of what had taken place, but I decided against doing so, as a far worse fate would await us by informing them of a murder that had taken place between members of our own squad. I am writing these notes on my cellphone as I walk to my determined location in the hopes that if something happens to me, the truth will need to be known…

THE APOCALYPSE HAS BEGUN

THE APOCALYPSE HAS BEGUN

To everyone I know, this is my farewell, as soon, they will find me.

My name is Patrick Ellingson. I am a level A, the head-conducting scientist in the R/717 Program. To whoever may find this, please, find it in whatever power or way you can. Release the contents of this letter to the public, because the fate of us all is in the balance. As I am writing to you, at this moment, I am trying to find any way possible in which I can be successful in my task of passing this paper through.

The R/717 Program, presently, is conducted in Facility 2/913 since the Cold War, first making its inner-official approval in the year 1963. Facility 2/913 is located on the outskirts of Russia, whose location I will reveal after describing the events taking place. Through the former Soviet-U.S. Partnership Reform, we were able to continue the further development of our programs.

The R/717 Program revolves around the motoric functions of the human brain, delving deep into the central core of the matter tissue, and its relation with the remaining vital functions of the human body. My first assignment to this program happened in the year 1982. Since then, I have gained leveling promotions inside its rankings. This is the reason for my previously written of position.

The core aim, from what I had learned throughout the years before, was at first to investigate the overall relationship between the brain and the critical aspects involving the body's waking functions. Upon my first arrival, the then-leading engineer in the MACHINERY SECTOR R/717 was Miles Jefferson, a wise, loving figure, who has taught me both the moral, economic, and biological results which are the central pillars this program was seeking to achieve.

Now, I fear that after what has occurred yesterday, and what was, ultimately, being led up to become of this program ever since his passing, is becoming a reality. If passed onward, this reality will become our end.

Our first, what was thought at the times, great achievement, occurred on September 6th, 1999, when the MACHINERY SECTOR R/717 successfully achieved to connect the human brain to an oxygen tube, a brain, which was outside of the human body, and had managed to function as the then-developed hydropenic/sulfuric liquid mixed with DNA tissue was injected inside of its own.

The year 2004 marked our second breakthrough in the pursuit of accomplishing the goals of the R/717 Program. It was our team, which was still led by Jefferson, who was responsible for the achievement of the further written results. As the previous years had passed, hundreds of brains were further being passed through the same process of their interveinal connection without the presence of a human body. The age of the brains ranged from adults, taken from humans who were, at the very maximum capacity of our goals, in the late 40s age range, and going down to children whose categorical age was placed lowest to be the age of 6.

The breakthrough in question, the one that was achieved, was the given ability of the brain to be connected to a manual intake oxygen tube, and after further injecting it with testosterone gained from the testicles which had been in their final stages of life, it was deemed a success, as the brain was now able to willingly intake oxygen, which was mixed with several microglial elements needed for the organ's functioning.

Only two months after, Jefferson had passed away, and I was on his deathbed. That day, in his final moments, he assured me to continue in his footsteps, and to ensure, myself, that the ethical elements set in stone since the program's formation remain in their place.

Following the ongoing years, more than half a decade would pass before we would achieve our next accomplishment. The year 2012, to be more precise, the very month of December, was when we would achieve our greatest accomplishment yet. If questions were to arise, for whoever may find this letter if it safely leaves the facility, the years that had parted the previous, and the one I am writing of now, have been packed with many developments in the containing elements of the liquid that had been called RS707, as well as several ongoing developments in the process of, firstly implementing, then distancing from the machines that were used to disperse it inside the brain's tissue.

The year written above was when we would have gained the ability, to, frankly speaking in as simple wording as can be thought of, to essentially allow the brain, which was still connected to the interveinal tubes, to disperse functioning properties to the organs that had been taken out of our subjects, in result, enabling them to independently function without the need of the body.

2016 was the year when I had gained the promotion to the position I now hold, and it also was the year when the next breakthrough in the program was about to take place, further passing into January 2017, when it had been successfully realized.

The brain that had belonged to Subject 178342, was the first that would receive the then drastically altered version of the liquid, and it was the first that had still been connected to the remaining organs crucial for the functioning of the human body, but was disconnected from the interveinal tubes which were needed for it to live on.

All the performed testings were deemed to become negative, as the intended result was not achieved in December 2016. The organs, as well as the brain itself, were placed inside the 045 Control Room, and were set to be dispatched to the highest bidder who needed them for the requesting customers in the darknet market, as the bidding was set to commence in February 2017.

January 17th was when the breakthrough occurred. As, outside of our understanding, the brain, which was preserved in the humid vapor-mixed temperature of the room, began to function. Upon further inspection, the organs had all functioned accordingly, and that is when changes were beginning to erupt within our order.

This event was incredible, and it marked a phenomenal achievement in the accomplishment of the R/717 Program, but with its sudden appearance, several men and women within our ranks were changing their views in which direction the further research should proceed.

I remembered well what Jefferson had asked me to do, and I was doing my best to keep the ethical standards in place, but as time had passed on, the inevitable outcome was not going in our group's way.

This brings us to yesterday.

TEST 717-996

The core foundation of this test was to inject the liquid into the brain of a person who had still been alive, and the subject that had been chosen was Tymothy Granger, 21 years old, born in England.

The subject was placed in a deep state of unconsciousness, during which the liquid had been inserted. The time period that needed to pass was placed to match the 66 days, which, at first, had passed in the first breakthrough, and the further testings after.

After its passage, Tymothy manually awakened and was placed in the 996 Control Room, where the left-wing conductor, Mandis Wallar, stood in front of him. The young man was unable to move and was placed in a standing position, as several nerve pausing agents were inserted inside his motoric functions. As the order came, Mandis pulled out the pistol he was holding in his right holster and fired several bullets into Tymothy's body, following the key order to not fire in the head.

The young man fell onto the ground as blood poured out of his body, leaving him lying in a pool of blood. That is when it happened. Exactly after 3 minutes and 47 seconds, the young man's body rose. Our teams watched in bewilderment as the operating conductor ordered Mandis to walk closer to him and check for his sense of sight. As the left-wing conductor walked closer, and was now standing in front of him, we noticed that just now, Tymothy's eyes began to open. And, that is when the event I speak of now, had occurred.

In the blink of a second, Tymothy lunged his teeth inside Mandis's neck, leading to a splash of blood to land on the see-through windowed wall, and as the conductor fell to the ground, Tymothy continued to further bite into his skin and was consuming the contents inside.

Immediately, several armed personnel walked inside, firing bullets that had ultimately put the man down, but not before we noticed the increased agility Tymothy now held, as the young man quickly jumped onto one soldier, striking him down.

Today, on November 2nd, 2019, we received an order from the upper levels. We must continue to perform the same experiment on dozens of people, and as of this moment, preparations are being made for us to place groups of subjects inside the control rooms, to further examine, as the needed time period passes, how they will behave when standing next to each other, and from what we ha been told, the numbers will only keep becoming bigger, all until, an experiment is performed in an outside environment…

If you are reading this letter, and are standing outside of our location, I beg you to make this known worldwide as quickly as possible, for if not, terrible things may come, events… I hope not to see in ours, or the lifetimes ahead…

BARTON INDUSTRIES: RESEARCH SECTOR

PATRICK ELLINGSON

I SEE THE FUTURE IN MY DREAMS

I SEE THE FUTURE IN MY DREAMS

I woke up today. But as I had wished before, I would be grateful if I had not. My name is Kenneth Roland, and I see the future in my dreams.

How do I do that? The sarcastic or suspicious bunch of you might ask, but there would be no answer I could give you.

To begin, I will tell you shortly about myself, where I live, and what type of person I am. As I have written, my name is Kenneth Roland, and I am the current governor of the state of New York. The sole reason as to why I am writing this to you is not because I have gotten a hunch or a feeling for the need of someone to read my story. Rather, it is something else. My reign over this area will no longer last.

I have been summoned by the council, and upon my latest attendance, the major vote was brought that I best be transported to the Safe Ground, where I will be supposed to live the rest of my days, like the others who are present there before my expected arrival.

But I know that like them, I will not make it, as long before I board the craft, I will be terminated, an action which was spoken by many to truly occur.

What I am writing in this report, I ask you to take in each word, each event as carefully is possible. If not, then I fear there will be no way of stopping what is yet to come.

The future, it had not revealed itself to me in a brief time span. I cannot recall the date, but I am certain these events began to occur nineteen years ago.

Back then, I was finishing the college I was assigned to graduate, as the family which I had been, and still am a part of, did not give me, or my brothers and sister, the ability to obtain the freedom of choice.

Even now, when my end comes near, I cannot share with you the real term of events that are set to happen with our community, as all of us, down to every single one, are expected to listen, and to obey under every command passed down from the top of our Party.

But know this, whatever we are set to do, we must, not because we may necessarily want to, but because we need to in order to proceed with the overall plan for the future set by our chain of command.

This sole reason is why, when I began encountering these dreams, the first set of choices I had made was to contact and to report to my handlers what I am experiencing, who, after hearing me speak of the events I dreamt of, simply chuckled, and had assured me not to have any need of worry, as the commanding level of our, or the areas above, had no plan or reason to perform its realization.

This dream, the first one, had involved an event you all should know of, as well as remember, for a long time to come. The event I speak of is the falling of the World Trade Center, an event that had occurred on September 11th.

On the day of its occurrence, I was immediately called by my handlers, who informed me the upper levels of our Order requested my sudden arrival. On that very meeting, and going onward, the Order had insisted on the expected report of any dreams that may come, and until now, all of them had come to pass.

The events I dreamt of involved the invasion of Iraq which had been performed by the combined troops, the terroristic attack of London, the one that had occurred in the year 2005, the Arab Spring, the raid of Pakistan in 2011, the Syrian Civil War, the bombing of the Boston Marathon, the voting of Britain to leave the European Union, and the one which I tell you of now.

Many of these events did not involve, as far as I was allowed to know, the developing decisions made by the upper levels of our Party, and their happenings, all of them, to the very first one, had all corresponded to what I had dreamt, although, I could not define the clear basis of their location or cause, which has led to their inevitable realization.

The event I am about to describe involves the future of the entire world. I saw it in ruins. Europe, Asia, The United States, all of them crumbling, and the reason itself, has not yet been revealed to me, but it involved the vision of something terrible.

I saw millions of decayed humans, who seemed to be dead, their body parts falling apart, but they were roaming the Earth, walking through streets that were themselves destroyed by what could only seem to be the strength of war.

As I confessed to them, my handlers, what I had seen, they instructed me to remain in my current position and await further orders.

Now, I find myself in my office, whose position has been set for a sudden vote by the people of New York, and the votes of men and women who will try to refute the will of the Party. But as many have ended before, so will they end in what is intended to be declared.

I...I do not know why... I am even writing this... but I know it in myself, and I ask it of anyone who may find this note... Spread the knowledge of these events to the public, and... and maybe... someone will know their meaning...

Farewell...

THE OTHER SIDE

THE OTHER SIDE

SUBJECT NAME: ELIZABETH WARREN

INTERVIEW ID: 34971

INTERROGATOR: JOSHUA EDDISON

Joshua: "My warm greetings, Mrs. Warren."

Elizabeth: "And a warm regard to you, Joshua."

Joshua: "I think the best way we could begin is if you were to introduce yourself to our audience. Tell us about yourself, where are you from, what type of work do you do, and where we are located now."

Elizabeth: "Certainly, Joshua. Can I begin?"

Joshua: "Yes, of course."

Elizabeth: "Well, for everyone who may be listening, or reading this report, I... I don't know if we'll get any television coverage, hah. But allow me to introduce myself clearly. Oh Lord, Joshua, can we do this line again? I do not think I have done it very well."

Joshua: "Sure thing, Mrs. Warren, our editing staff will ensure the previous line is cut. Yes, Michael, once we're done, you and Thomas are cutting the previous line, as well as mine now. Are we clear? Good, Mrs. Warren, you may begin once more."

Elizabeth: "I send my warmest regards to everyone who may witness this interview, in whatever shape or form. My name is Elizabeth Warren, and I am speaking to you from what some would say is a location found deep in the woods of central North Carolina, about 50 miles south of Greensboro. Upon hearing these words, you may know what it is I speak of, and you would likely be correct to guess. I am addressing you from my newly built wooden home, a two-story L-shaped house built on a site known as the Devil's Tramping Ground."

Joshua: "Just to cut you off for a sec. Folks, Mrs. Warren is addressing the Devil's Tramping Ground, the recently famous circle where time itself has witnessed that no plant or tree will grow on its grounds, and as wandering hunters would tell you from their experiences, nor will any animals cross its path."

Elizabeth: "Which, you will find, Joshua, is a silly thing to say."

Joshua: "Well, Mrs. Warren, as both I and my two current colleagues can see, we have a beautiful flower in the corner behind you."

Elizabeth: "Oh that's… that's the one I bought yesterday. I sure hope it'll work this time."

Joshua: "Wh-"

Elizabeth: "Anyway, to continue. My name, which I have told you before, but will repeat, is Elizabeth Warren. And as of this exact moment, I am 72 years old, which, as my grandkids would tell me, is a heck of a long time to be here! I am a widowed woman, as my husband Eric, bless his soul, has passed away about a year and a half ago."

Joshua: "Excuse me for interrupting, but could you tell us more about him?"

Elizabeth: "Oh, Eric, sweetie."

Joshua remained silent, waiting for the woman to continue.

Elizabeth: "Oh, God!"

Joshua: "Uh, folks, we're going to take a momentary pause for a minute, and we'll be back shortly. Michael, turn it off, will you?"

Joshua: "We return once again and are now continuing to involve you in the story. Mrs. Warren, shall we continue?"

Elizabeth: "Oh, yes, of course, dear. Anyway, where was I?"

Joshua: "You were telling us about your husband, Eric."

Elizabeth: "Yes, Eric, he was a great soul. He has never, ever abandoned me, and if it were not for his sudden passing, the two of us would still be here, together."

Joshua: "Alright. Can you continue to tell us more about yourself?"

Elizabeth: "Yes. My name is Elizabeth. Oh yes! Elizabeth Warren, and I am 72 years old! A point which, as my grandkids would tell me, is a heck of a long time to be here! I am a widowed woman, as my husband Eric, Lord bless his soul..."

Joshua: "Uh, that is good for now. Thank you, Elizabeth. Can I address you by your name? Is that okay with you?"

Elizabeth: "Oh, yes, of course, sweetie."

Joshua: "So, can you tell us what has been happening here for the past few months? Can you introduce our audience to the reason we were called to arrive here?"

Elizabeth: "Oh, well, it's those damn folks, the folks who wander around my property, harassing me!"

Joshua: "Well, as we have told you before, they were the ones who called us here. They believe there are events they have witnessed occurring which need our attention. What is your response to that?"

Elizabeth: "They are jealous of me and my family! They want us out of here, so they can use our property for themselves! A bunch of loonies, hah, if I were to tell you, they are!"

Joshua: "Well, before we jump to any conclusions, Mrs. Warren, I want you to hear what Mr. Thomas has to say, as he is a man of God, and he wants to tell us what events are reported to be taking place here. Thomas, you can proceed."

Thomas: "It is a pleasure to be here, Mrs. Elizabeth. For those listening, my name is Thomas Forrester, and I am a specialized priest who was contacted by your host, Joshua Eddison. Mrs. Elizabeth, the events that have been reported to take place around your home seem to report that every night the local hunters were in the close vicinity of this area, at 2 to 3 AM, loud feminine screams are heard to be coming from within your walls. What is your response to that?"

Elizabeth: "Oh, honey, those are just made up loonies."

Thomas: "To continue further, except for these sounds, many others are reported to be heard. Several of them are reported by over six different hunters to resemble a faint ringing of bells which is heard to be coming from the yard around, but as they pass through the thickness to see, nothing remains to be in front of their view, and the sounds cease to continue once their eyes are met with your outer surroundings."

Elizabeth: "They lie. They want to take everything from me! Didn't I tell you that?"

Thomas: "Yes, you have, Mrs. Elizabeth. But here is where I want our conversation to lead. These two types of events are not the only ones that have come to our attention. And this is where I want you to tell your answer after I finish. Hunter Randy Larsh has spoken to me personally before I arrived here today, and he swore on everything he had that four days ago, he could see several figures standing behind some of your curtain-drawn windows, and two of them, he could not, and still cannot explain, as their features seem to haunt him ever since the sighting. What is your response to that?"

Elizabeth: "Oh, well, those are likely to be my grandkids! Have I told you about my grandkids?"

Thomas: "Mrs. Warren, your grandkids reside in a different state, one passing a few days-long distance from your location."

Joshua: "Hold on, Thomas, we don't want to pressure Mrs. Warren. Don't we?"

Elizabeth: "But they are right here, with us."

Thomas: "Where, Mrs. Elizabeth?"

Elizabeth: "Well, Jason is standing right behind you."

Joshua: "Mrs. Warren, no one is here with us. You must have gotten confused for a bit, but don't you worry, we'll get everything sorted out."

Elizabeth: "You better keep quiet now, young man! Eric, my dear, put it down!"

Thomas: "Elizabeth, who do you see?"

Elizabeth: "Oh, no! No! No! No! The mean man is here! No I don't want to…"

Joshua: "What do you not want, Elizabeth?"

Elizabeth: "He, he wants me to pass you something…"

Thomas: "Mrs. Warren, what would that be?"

Elizabeth: "A… a message…"

Joshua: "Um, we… we would be happy to hear it… What is it, Mrs. Warren?"

Elizabeth: "You… you are… you are all… going to die… YOU ARE ALL GOING TO DIE!"

MISTER BARTON

MISTER BARTON

I saw him. Today was the day when I would finally meet him.

My name is Daniel Allengson, and I am a court investigator who specializes in discovering, and inevitably, judging potential fraud made in the business of foreign affairs. I am writing to you hoping these notes may be found, and that needed action may be taken, in which I hope I will be freed. Only then will I be able to tell the truth.

My assignment had been given by my supervising judge, Ted Clark, who was battling a month-long internal conflict with the legal representatives of Barton Industries. The trial that had been taking place involved the accusation which was placed against Barton Industries: Public Relations, where the judge had a relationship with one of its employees, Laura Reilly, who had contacted him hoping to receive critical information she believed had possessed the ability to harm the integrity of the federal law placed against foreign businesses which had partnered with the ones located inside of the United States.

The employee called Ted on his private phone in the middle of the night, where he witnessed her pleading for his action, as Laura was accusing the organization she worked for to be involved in a potential breaking of the law stationed to hold the integrity of the voting process located inside her State, as the counting of the then received ballots was taking place inside of the building Barton Industries was providing for the government as a further extension to the overall partnership between this private corporation and the State itself.

The witnessing Ted had received spoke of a process which involved the fraudulent creation of new ballots which were aimed to provide assistance to the underperforming candidate, who himself was tight in the race with his opponent for the gain of votes the State would provide to whoever would win the majority of its votes.

The process had taken the length of a time-span that surpassed the length of several months, and over its passing, Ted had taken a substantial lead in the reveal of the then passed elections, which I will not write of due to private reasons if this note does indeed find its way through.

That is when Ted had contacted me to perform the task of internally searching the retrieved ballots which had been placed inside the facility, although the elections had been set in stone. And I was honestly preparing to do that, but not long after, I was contacted by my partnering overlookers, who had ordered me to not proceed with Ted's request, as they will arrange that a more suitable candidate, who will protect the safety of the public outcry, will appeal to the request Barton Industries had placed for the count to not be changed.

But, I guess, judgment had kicked in, and I told them I will be the one who will proceed, no matter what, and that I will make sure the true count will be revealed to the nation, no matter the consequences it may place in the increase of ongoing suspicion directed towards the current government's elects.

As the days had passed, and the date of my appearance at the facility was coming closer, I received a phone call in which I heard my dear wife Samantha calling for me to help her. Someone had kidnapped her.

Personnel working within an undisclosed sector stationed under the umbrella of Barton Industries ordered me to arrive at the facility found in a location that I will not myself disclose due to the concern of the safety my wife now has.

That is when I met him, Mr. Barton himself, standing in front of me with no one else in sight, as the door I was led through, which was located in the complex corridors of the building, was now closed.

He did not look right.

His eyes, they were black. His voice, it sounded as if a machine was developing it as it had exited his mouth.

The words he spoke revealed many things I was not aware of, and that is when his skin had peeled itself off his entire body, melting with the suit, revealing what his true appearance was.

I...I know that I will never be freed, as what I know now, will not see the light of day...

Mr. Barton... he is not human... he is-

AUTHOR CONTACT

Dear reader, I thank you for picking up and reading "We Are So Sorry". It is with my sincere thoughts that I hope you have enjoyed the story you have read.

However, if there are elements you might have not enjoyed, or perhaps, elements you would like to find out more about, I invite you to contact me through the following contact details, where we can engage in many future conversations.

As always, I would truly be grateful for your review on Amazon & other retailers this book is available on. A review from a reader like you means the world to me.

MY PERSONAL E-MAIL ADDRESS: stipelozina@stipelozina.com

Made in the USA
Columbia, SC
07 February 2023

11094116R00041